Go, Wendall, Go!

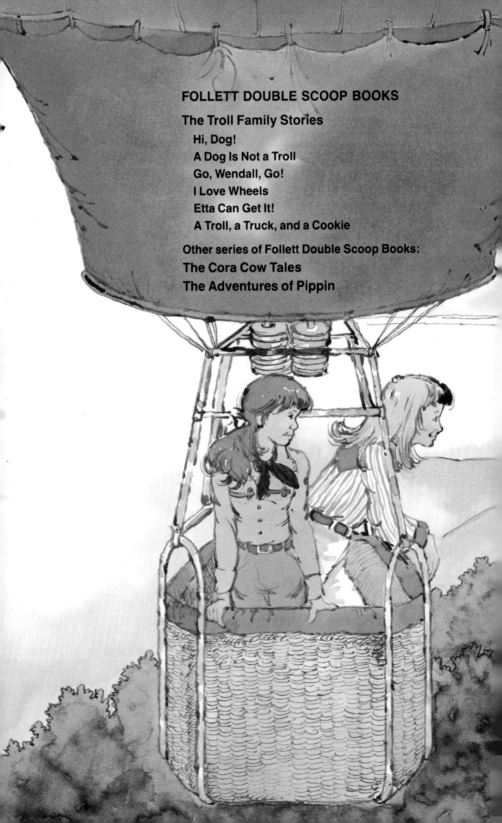

FOLLETT DOUBLE SCOOP BOOKS

Go, Wendall, Go!

Phylliss Adams
Eleanore Hartson
Mark Taylor

Illustrated by Dennis Hockerman

Follett Publishing Company
Chicago, Illinois

Atlanta, Georgia • Dallas, Texas
Sacramento, California • Warrensburg, Missouri

LC 81–17415
ISBN 0–695–41614–6
ISBN 0–695–31614–1 (pbk.)

"Wendall, you work and work,"
said Leona.
"I want you to play."

"Play?" said Wendall.

"Play!" said Buddy and Blossom.

"You want to work, Wendall,"
said Etta.
"Go and work."

6

"Hi!" said Blossom and Buddy.

"Hi, hi, hi."

9

"Go, Blossom, go!" said Buddy.

10

"A red balloon!" said Wendall.
"A balloon can go up.
A balloon can come down."

11

"See this balloon!" said Wendall.
"A balloon is not for work.
A balloon is for play.
And I want to play."

12

"Look, Leona," said Wendall.
"See this balloon go up!"

"Wendall!" said Leona.
"Can the balloon come down?"

13

"Wendall, come down," said Leona.
"Dandy Dog and I want you down!"

16

"I can not come down,"
said Wendall.

17

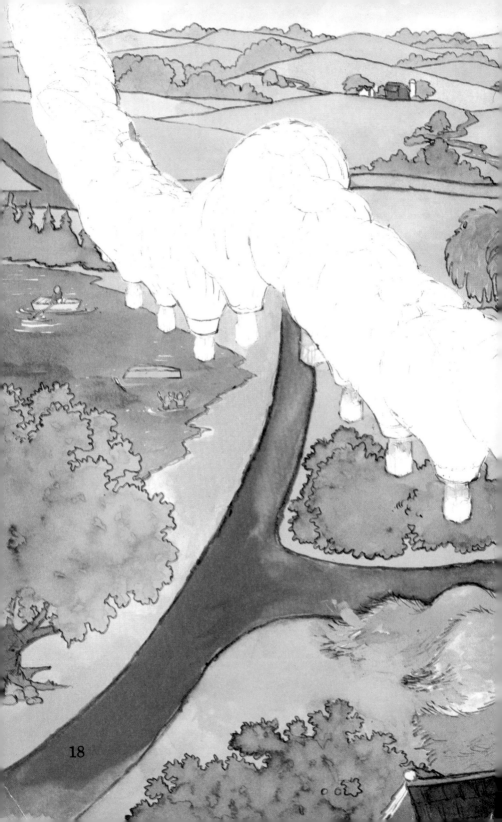

The red balloon is up.
The red balloon is down.
And Wendall is up and down.

"Hi!" said Wendall.

The balloon is down!
Is Wendall down?

"Wendall, I see you can play,"
said Etta.

"I <u>can</u> play," said Wendall.
"I can!
I can!"

The Troll Word Book

come   Dandy Dog can <u>come</u> to Buddy.

down   Blossom can come <u>down</u>.

go   See Etta <u>go</u>.

If necessary, read these directions to the child:
Read the words and sentences.

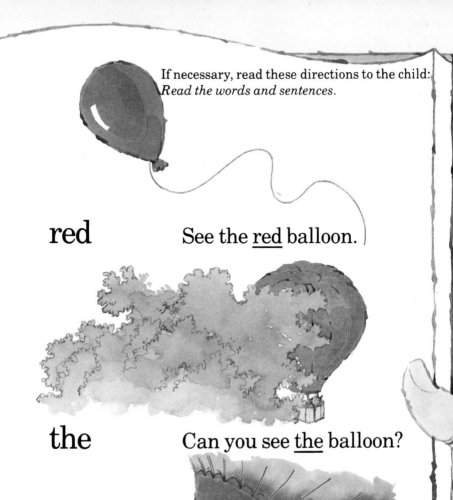

red   See the <u>red</u> balloon.

the   Can you see <u>the</u> balloon?

up   Wendall and Leona go <u>up</u>.

I See

B b

D d

W w

L l

29

Sky Fun

With your finger trace a way to the troll house, but do not touch a cloud. Start at the balloon. Go to the plane. Next go to the helicopter. Then find the troll house.

Go, Wendall, Go! is the third book of the Troll Family Stories for beginning readers. All words used in the story are listed here. (The words in darker print were introduced in this book. The other words were introduced in earlier books.)

a	Etta	Leona	**the**
and	for	look	this
balloon	**go**	not	to
Blossom	hi	play	**up**
Buddy	I	**red**	want
can	is	said	Wendall
come		see	work
Dandy Dog			you
down			

About the Authors

Phylliss Adams, Eleanore Hartson, and Mark Taylor have a combined background that includes writing books for children and teachers, teaching at the elementary and university levels, and working in the areas of curriculum development, reading instruction and research, teacher training, parent education, and library and media services.

About the Illustrator

Since his graduation from Layton School of Art in Milwaukee, Wisconsin, Dennis Hockerman has concentrated primarily on art for children's books, magazines, greeting cards, and games.

The artist lives and works in his home in Mequon, Wisconsin, with his wife and two children. The children enjoyed many hours in their dad's studio watching as the Troll Family characters came to life.